MATT CHRISTOPHER®

THE EXTREME TEAM

#4
ON THIN ICE

Text by Stephanie Peters
Illustrated by Michael Koelsch

LITTLE, BROWN AND COMPANY
New York ~ Boston

Little, Brown and Company

Time Warner Book Group
1271 Avenue of the Americas, New York, NY 10020
Visit our Web site at www.lb-kids.com

First Edition

The characters and events portrayed in this book are fictitious. Any similarity to real persons, living or dead, is coincidental and not intended by the author.

Matt Christopher® is a registered trademark of Catherine M. Christopher.

Library of Congress Cataloging-in-Publication Data
Peters, Stephanie True.
On thin ice / text by Stephanie Peters ; illustrated by Michael Koelsch. — 1st ed.
p.   cm. — (The extreme team ; #4)
"Matt Christopher."
Summary: Savannah is excited about throwing a holiday ice skating party and has already invited friends from her new school, when she learns that Jonas has invited the crowd from her old school to a party the same day.
ISBN 0-316-73756-9 (hc) / ISBN 0-316-73739-9 (pb)
[1. Parties — Fiction.   2. Friendship — Fiction.]
I. Koelsch, Michael, ill.   II. Christopher, Matt.
III. Title.   IV. Series.
PZ7.P441833On 2004   2003052096
[Fic] — dc22

10   9   8   7   6   5   4   3   2   1

WOR (hc)

COM-MO (pb)

Printed in the United States of America

CHAPTER ONE

Savannah Smith sat at her desk, chin in hand, staring at the fat snowflakes falling past the window. *I wonder if the hill will be ready for snowboarding soon,* she thought. *That would make Bizz happy.* Belicia "Bizz" Juarez was Savannah's best friend. She was helping Savannah learn to snowboard.

Savannah wished for the thousandth time that she and Bizz attended the same school. But this September, Savannah had started at a private, all-girls school called the Academy. Bizz went to their old school.

Savannah missed seeing Bizz and her other friends every day. But her father wouldn't hear of her switching schools. "You'll get a wonderful education at the Academy," he said. "And you'll still get to see Bizz after school and on the weekends. Plus, you'll make new friends at the Academy."

Luckily, Savannah *had* started to become friends with a few girls. One girl in particular, Angela Sturgess, had gone out of her way to make Savannah feel welcome. Angela was very different from Bizz. Bizz loved extreme sports, especially roller hockey. Angela preferred quieter activities, like arts and crafts. Savannah enjoyed art projects, too, but she also liked blading and boarding with Bizz at the local skatepark. She sometimes wondered how Angela and Bizz would get along if they met.

The bell rang, signaling the end of the school week. Savannah joined the throng of girls in the hallway.

"Hey, Savannah! Wait up!" It was Angela. Savannah paused until the pretty blond girl caught up to her. "I got your party invitation."

"Wow, that was quick!" Savannah and her family

were hosting a holiday ice-skating party for Savannah's classmates and their parents. Mr. Smith had installed a rink in the backyard earlier that year. People could skate until it got dark, then they could come inside for refreshments. Invitations to the party had gone out only a few days before.

Savannah had thought about inviting Bizz and her other friends to the party, too. But when she tried to imagine her Academy classmates hanging out with them, she couldn't. Besides, she knew her old friend Jonas Malloy would have a party. He always did. So in the end, she hadn't invited Bizz and the others to the skating party. In fact, she hadn't even told them about it. Not yet, anyway.

"It's so cool that you have a skating rink in your backyard," Angela was saying. "Could I skate on it someday?"

"Sure!" Savannah replied. "Ask your mom if you can come over tomorrow afternoon."

The two girls joined the other students waiting for their parents to pick them up. "The invitation says to bring a present to exchange," Angela said. "Does that mean one present for each of our classmates or just one present only?"

"Just one present only," Savannah confirmed. "We'll do a grab-bag swap."

"What's that?"

"Each kid brings a present and puts it into a big box. Then everyone gets a number. Number one picks a present from the box and opens it. Then number two picks a present and opens it. If number two wants to keep her present, she can, or she can trade her present for number one's present. And so on until everyone's picked and traded."

"Seems like number one gets a raw deal," Angela said.

"Actually, it's good to be number one," said Savannah, "because once everyone's picked, number one does the last trade, so she gets to pick from all the gifts!"

"Ooh, then I hope I get to be number one!"

CHAPTER TWO

Mrs. Smith drove up a moment later. Savannah got into the car, waved good-bye to Angela, and settled into the backseat. Plows had cleared most of the snow from the streets, so she and her mother made it home in no time. The phone was ringing when they walked into the house.

"Hey, girlfriend!" Bizz bellowed from the other end. "Grab your board and meet us at the skate-park!"

"My board?" Savannah replied. "Are you crazy? There must be at least six inches of snow on the ground!"

Bizz laughed. "Not your *skate*board, your *snow*-board! Alison called to say the hill behind the park is open for business!"

Alison Lee was a teenager in charge of the local skatepark. She made sure the kids who were skate-boarding, inline skating, and snowboarding were be-ing careful. Savannah knew that if Alison said it was okay to snowboard today, then the conditions were just right.

"I'll meet you there!"

Twenty minutes later, her mother dropped her off in the parking lot. Savannah joined a parade of kids climbing the hill. She had just reached the top when *thwap!* a snowball smacked into her stomach. She looked up to see Xavier "X" McSweeney grinning at her. Jonas Malloy and Bizz were behind him.

"Yo, Savannah!" Jonas said. "When are you going to get yourself some proper snowboarding gear? You know, goggles and a face thingy like mine." He tugged his fleece face warmer into place so that only his eyes were peeking out. These he covered with yellow-tinted goggles.

"Forget him," X said. "You're just in time to see my first revert of the season."

"Don't make a big hole in the snow when you do a plant!" Jonas joked.

"Ha!" X snorted. "If I fall, I'll eat my hat." With a wave, he took off, zigzagging his way down the hill. When he'd gone halfway, he suddenly twisted around one hundred and eighty degrees. Then he rode the rest of the hill backward. Bizz and Jonas cheered.

"That's a revert?" Savannah said. "Switching from forward to backward?"

"Forward to *fakie,*" Jonas corrected. "Yep, that's it. Wanna give it a try?"

Savannah shook her head. "I'm still a newbie at this stuff. It's cruiser runs for me all the way."

"I'm with you!" Bizz agreed. She flung an arm around Savannah's shoulders. Savannah grinned and put an arm around Bizz, too.

"Great shot! Say cheese!" Bizz and Savannah looked up to see Alison pointing a camera at them. "I'm taking photos to hang on the wall of the Community Center," Alison told them as she snapped their picture. "'Friends to the end,' that's what I'll label this one. Now get a move on. You're holding up the line!"

Bizz didn't hesitate. She strapped herself on to her board, gave a little hop, and took off down the slope. Savannah watched her friend go, then secured her bindings and followed Bizz down the hill.

Friends to the end, she thought. *That's Bizz and me, all right!*

CHAPTER THREE

Savannah was still new to snowboarding, so she *swished* down the slope nice and easy, getting used to the feel of the snowboard. She had to pinwheel her arms a few times to stay upright. Otherwise, her first run of the winter felt great.

She caught up with Bizz at the bottom. As they stepped out of their bindings, they saw Charlie Abbott and Mark Goldstein with X.

"Hey, guys!" Bizz called. "Wait for —"

Floosh! A wall of snow covered Bizz and Savannah. Jonas had just finished his run. He'd ended it by digging his board into the snow sideways, lifting the white powder into the air.

"Get him!" Bizz yelled. She scooped up some snow and heaved it at Jonas. Savannah and the others did the same. Then, following some unspoken signal, X and Jonas teamed up, Charlie and Mark turned on Savannah and Bizz — and the snowball fight turned into a three-way battle.

After a few breathless minutes, Savannah dove behind a snowbank for protection. She lay still for a moment, then risked a peek.

Bizz, X, Charlie, Jonas, and Mark jumped up from behind the other side of the bank. Each had a huge armload of snow. Savannah ducked inside her coat, but her friends moved faster. She shrieked as snow hit her neck and trickled down her back.

"Seriously, girl, you gotta get a face warmer thingy. It protects your neck, too," Jonas advised. Then he hurled himself over the snowbank. The others followed, howling with laughter.

"Smile for the camera!"

Still grinning, the kids looked up just as Alison

snapped a photo. She took two more shots, then tucked her camera safely inside her coat pocket.

"If you guys want to do any more runs, you'd better stop clowning around," Alison said. "The sun's going down. I have to close the hill soon."

Without another word, Savannah and the others scrambled up, grabbed their boards, and rushed to the top of the hill. They each got in three more runs before Alison called an end to boarding for the day.

Tired and happy, Savannah tromped with her friends to the parking lot. Looking at their smiling faces, she felt a wave of guilt for keeping her skating party a secret. *I'm going to invite them after all!* she thought. *They're my oldest friends and I want them there!*

She opened her mouth to speak, when Jonas suddenly smacked his forehead. "I almost forgot!" he said. "My dad's finally got our party planned. Get this: We're going bowling! The bowling alley is putting in one of his video games next week. The owner said we could have a couple of lanes."

Mr. Malloy had the coolest job ever. He was a video-game designer. He got to work at home, thinking up fun games for kids — and adults — to play. Some, like the one that was going into the bowling alley, were made for arcades.

"We can bowl and play his video game for a few hours," Jonas continued, "then go to my house for the Christmas party!"

"Ahem," Mark Goldstein cleared his throat.

"Sorry, Mark, I mean the *holiday* party," Jonas amended. "You can bring your dreidel and show us how to play Hanukkah games. We can exchange gifts, too. Okay?"

"Gifts? What makes you think I wanna give you a gift?" Bizz punched Jonas in the shoulder.

"Back off, or I'm returning what I got you," Jonas warned. Bizz held up her hands in mock terror.

The talk of gifts reminded Savannah of her

school skating party. "Jonas, when's your party?" she asked.

"Saturday, December 15, at three o'clock. The lanes are reserved for two hours."

Savannah's heart sank. Jonas's party was the same day and time as her Academy party!

CHAPTER FOUR

While the other kids chatted excitedly about Jonas's party, Savannah remained silent. She knew she should tell them she couldn't go, but she couldn't get the words out. How could she? She hadn't told them about the Academy skating party. She tried to imagine telling them now, maybe even inviting them to come by after the bowling party. But somehow, she didn't think that would go over so well. They'd want to know why they hadn't been invited to the *real* party. And Savannah knew she wasn't ready to explain *that*. She was glad when her mother finally pulled in.

Bizz poked her head inside the door. "Hi, Mrs. Smith!" she said. "Can Savannah come snowboarding again tomorrow?"

"Hello, Bizz. Not in the morning," Savannah's mother replied. "She and I are going Christmas shopping."

"Well, I certainly don't want to stop you from doing that, just in case you're getting something for someone special!" Bizz waggled her eyebrows and grinned. "But can she come tomorrow afternoon?"

Mrs. Smith laughed. "If she wants to, it's fine with me!"

Savannah was eating her breakfast the next morning when the phone rang. It was Angela.

"My mom says I can come over to skate this afternoon," she said happily.

Savannah had completely forgotten she'd invited Angela to her house. She couldn't very well cancel those plans, even though it meant she couldn't go snowboarding with Bizz after all. She thought about

telling Angela that the rink was still covered with snow, but a peek out the kitchen window showed that her father had already cleared it. She couldn't lie to her new friend, so she told Angela to come by after lunch.

After she hung up, she called Bizz to let her know she wouldn't be snowboarding that day. She got the answering machine.

"Um, Bizz, I can't meet you at the hill," she said. "I, um, I'm not sure if I'll be home from shopping in time. I'll call you later, okay?"

She and her mother left after breakfast to start their Christmas shopping at the mall. Savannah looked at toys, books, CDs, and jewelry. But nothing she saw seemed quite right for the gift swap.

"Let's go to the craft store," Savannah's mother finally said. "Maybe we'll find something there."

The craft store was one of Savannah's favorite places. Any time she had money to spend, that's where she went. Savannah spied the perfect gift the minute they walked in. It was a bulb-planting kit.

The kit came with a bowl, special paints, a bag of white stones, and five bulbs. You painted the bowl, then filled it with the stones. When the paint was dry, you added water and planted the bulbs in the stones. In a few weeks, the bulbs sprouted roots and, later, green shoots and flowers. In the spring, you planted the bulbs in the ground. If you were lucky, the flowers grew again the next year.

Savannah thought it would be cool to have flowers in the winter. She hoped one of her classmates would think so, too. She carried the kit to the counter and pulled money from her pocket to pay. The kit cost a little more than she'd planned to spend, but she thought it was worth it.

Suddenly, as she reached for the bag, Savannah realized she'd just spent most of her savings on the kit. Where was she going to get the money to buy presents for Bizz and the others?

CHAPTER FIVE

When they got home, Savannah hurried to her room
to count the money remaining in her piggy bank.
There wasn't much left. She thought about asking
her mother for an advance on her allowance, but
since she didn't know what she was going to get Bizz
and the others, she didn't know how much to ask for.
What if it wasn't enough and she had to ask for more
later? Sighing, she put the money back in the bank
and went to the kitchen for lunch. Her mother was
on the phone in her office, but she'd left a sandwich
on the table for her.

Angela showed up just after Savannah finished

eating. She was dressed in a skater's outfit — a little skirt with a matching sweater, sparkling tights, and fluffy white earmuffs and mittens. Her hair was pulled back in a tight bun with a bow.

"Don't you have a skating outfit?"

Savannah looked down at her leggings and warm sweater and shrugged. "This is what I always wear. It's comfortable."

The girls put on their skates and stepped onto the rink. Angela struck off for the far end, then swooped back and grabbed Savannah's hand. "This is unbelievable!" she cried happily.

"I'll say," a new voice remarked.

Startled, Savannah whirled around. Bizz was standing near the rink, skates in hand. She stared at Savannah and Angela, still hand-in-hand on the rink.

Savannah dropped Angela's hand and skated over to Bizz. "What are you doing here?"

"I heard my mom talking to your mom on the phone, so I asked if I could come over. Your mom said to bring my skates. Guess she forgot to tell you I was coming." Bizz put her skates down and glanced at Angela. "Who's that?"

Angela introduced herself. "Do you know Savannah from the Academy, too?"

Bizz eyed the other girl's skating outfit. "No, I know Savannah because I'm her best friend. I'm Bizz."

"Oh," Angela said. She sized up Bizz's torn blue jeans and baggy sweatshirt.

Before Bizz had a chance to say anything else, Savannah pulled her to a bench. "I'm glad you're here! Let's do some skating, okay?" She handed Bizz her skates.

Bizz gave Angela another suspicious look, then laced up her skates and stepped onto the rink. "I haven't skated since last winter," she confessed. The words were barely out of her mouth when she fell hard on the ice.

Angela skated by and giggled. "Good thing you're wearing thick leg protection," she said, pointing at Bizz's blue jeans.

Bizz glared at her, then slowly stood up and started skating around the rink. As she got used to her skates, she picked up speed until she was a blur of movement. Finally, with a spray of ice chips, she came to a halt next to Savannah. "This rink is big enough for a game of hockey, you know," she said, breathing hard.

Angela skated to Savannah's other side. "Hockey? Who wants to watch a bunch of dumb boys play hockey?"

"It's better than figure skating," Bizz retorted. "Anyway, who said anything about watching? I'd play!"

"You would?" Angela shuddered. "I'd never play hockey. Would *you*, Savannah?"

"Yes, Savannah," Bizz asked, staring closely at her friend, "*would* you?"

Well, I guess I don't have to wonder how they'd get along if they ever met, Savannah thought dismally. *The answer is clear — badly!*

CHAPTER SIX

But it turned out that Savannah was wrong. At first, they all skated separately. Angela practiced spins, Bizz speed skated around the outside, and Savannah tried skating with one leg stretched out behind her. Then, slowly, they all started skating nearer to each other and saying things like "nice spin" and "wow, you're really fast." They had just begun playing follow-the-leader when Mr. Smith interrupted them.

"You girls look like you could use some hot chocolate," he called from the kitchen. "I'll bring some out."

As Savannah sipped her steaming mug of rich chocolate, she listened to Angela and Bizz talk about how great the rink was. Her hopes rose. Maybe they would wind up as friends after all. Her hopes were dashed a moment later.

"How was the mall this morning?" Bizz asked.

"Oh, were you shopping for the gift swap?" Angela asked.

Bizz looked at her. "What gift swap?"

"The gift swap we're doing at Savannah's big party," Angela said. "Aren't you coming to the party?"

Savannah wished the ground would open up and swallow her, that lightning would strike her in the head, that her father would call her inside – *anything* to keep from having to look at Bizz. Finally, though, she did risk a glance.

Bizz was staring at her, but when she spoke it was to Angela.

"I'm not sure. When is this big party happening again?" she asked. When Angela told her, Bizz gave a little snort. "Whaddya know. I've already been in-

vited to another party that same day. Too bad a person can't be in two places at once. Isn't it, Savannah?" Still wearing her skates, she grabbed her shoes and clumped out of the yard.

Savannah felt like she'd swallowed a lead balloon.

"Did I say something wrong?" Angela asked.

"No," Savannah answered miserably. "It's something I *didn't* say that's causing the problem."

That night at dinner, Savannah picked at her food.

"Is everything okay, Savannah?" her mother asked.

"Bizz hates me!" Savannah blurted out. She told her mother what had happened. "I should have told her and the others about the school party," she finished. "And now they're having their own party — without me." She put her head down on the table.

Her mother ruffled Savannah's thick black hair. "Poor baby. You know, the first step to making things right is to talk to your friends. Explain what happened. Why don't you give Bizz a call?"

But Savannah shook her head. "I doubt she'd talk to me tonight. I'll — I'll try her tomorrow."

"I'm sure everything will work out fine," her mother said.

Savannah hoped her mother was right — because she wasn't sure what she'd do if Bizz no longer wanted to be her "friend to the end."

CHAPTER SEVEN

Early the next morning, Savannah decided she'd better call Bizz before any more time passed. She dialed Bizz's number and held her breath. But instead of a person, she got the answering machine.

"I'll be at the slope this morning," she said after the machine's beep. "I — I hope I'll see you."

Mrs. Smith dropped off Savannah at the skatepark an hour later. It had snowed the night before, so there was a new blanket of powder on top of the old. The hill was already crowded with kids on sleds and snowboards. Savannah stood at the bottom, looking for Bizz and the others. When she didn't find them, she climbed the hill to ask Alison if they'd been there.

But Alison hadn't seen them. Savannah felt disappointment wash over her.

"Whoa, why the long face?" Alison said. "You look like you just lost your best friend."

"If I don't talk to Bizz soon, I just might!" Savannah exclaimed. She told Alison about the huge mess she'd made of things.

Alison listened sympathetically. "Girlfriend, that's a deep crater you've planted yourself in," she agreed. "But cheer up, I'll help you think of something to save the day. Meantime, why don't you do some runs?"

Savannah felt much better knowing that Alison was going to try to help her. So she strapped on her snowboard, pointed its nose downhill, and gave a little hop to get started. Knees bent and arms out for balance, she cut back and forth across the slope. The wind made her cheeks burn with cold and her eyes water.

Maybe Jonas was right about needing face and eye gear, she thought. She decided to add the items to her Christmas list. At the bottom of hill, she scanned the crowd once more. Still no sign of Bizz or the others. She trudged up the hill by herself.

After five more runs, Savannah was still alone. Her legs were tired and her toes were cold. But the ache inside her heart was worst of all. She could think of only one reason why her friends hadn't come snowboarding. Bizz had told them about the party — and knowing that Savannah was going to be at the hill that morning, they'd decided to stay away.

Alison *swooshed* up next to her. "I'm heading to the Community Center. Come thaw out with me."

The center lobby was decorated for the holidays. White lights twinkled on the walls, and paper snowflakes hung from the ceiling. One of the common rooms was decorated, too, but with balloons and streamers.

"A birthday party?" Savannah asked.

"A *surprise* birthday party," Alison corrected. "Those are the best kind, if you ask me. Who doesn't like being surprised?"

Savannah was about to answer when a collage of

photos on a nearby bulletin board caught her eye. She took a closer look. There, smack in the middle, was Alison's photo of Savannah and Bizz with their arms around each other. Next to that photo were the shots of the six friends after their snowball fight.

"Pretty good, huh?" Alison said, looking over Savannah's shoulder.

Savannah nodded. She stared at the photos, then at the twinkling lights and birthday-party decorations. An idea tickled the back of her brain.

"Alison," she said, "do you know if Bizz or the others have seen these yet?"

"I doubt it," Alison replied. "I just put them up this morning."

Savannah slowly smiled. "I think I've got a plan to make things right," she said. "Will you help me?"

CHAPTER EIGHT

As Savannah explained her idea, Alison nodded. "Dude, I think you've come up with a fab-o plan," she said. "I'll be back in a sec with what you need."

Alison returned a moment later and handed Savannah a small envelope. Savannah thanked her, then hurried to the parking lot. Her mother was due to pick her up any minute. When Mrs. Smith pulled in, Savannah gave her mother the envelope, stowed her snowboard in the trunk, and hopped into the backseat. Alison flashed her a thumbs-up as they pulled away.

"Mom, I know what to do about Bizz and the

others." On the ride home, Savannah described her idea to her mother.

"Savannah, that sounds great," her mother said. "Let's start working on it right when we get home." When they reached the house, Savannah ran to the phone and dialed a number. She crossed her fingers in hopes that the right person would answer.

He did. Savannah outlined her plan one more time. The person on the other end chuckled, then agreed to help in any way he could. Satisfied, Savannah hung up and turned to her mother with a grin.

"Would you mind taking me to the craft store again?" she asked. "I need some supplies for the presents." Her mother nodded, and Savannah hurried to empty her piggy bank of all the money she had left.

Getting supplies was easy. Making the presents would be harder — and she had only a week to prepare everything. School would take up most of that time, so she'd have to work quickly.

"Can't you drive any faster?" she urged her mother on the way home from the mall.

Her mother raised an eyebrow. "I could," she said, "but since you're out of money, you wouldn't be able to pay for the speeding ticket I'd get!"

For the next week, Savannah worked on her projects whenever she could. While she worked, she listened for the phone, hoping Bizz would call. She didn't. By Friday, Savannah wondered if her plan was going to work after all. She pushed the thought away.

It's got to work, she said to herself. *It's just got to!*

Saturday morning, Savannah ate a quick breakfast, then dressed to go outside. Her father was already at the rink.

"I know you're handy with scissors and paper," he said, "but how are you with hammers and nails?"

"Try me," Savannah said confidently.

So Mr. Smith handed her a tall, skinny board, a hammer, and some nails. "Space them out every five feet or so," he advised her. "Oh, and try not to hit your thumb!"

Grinning, Savannah knelt next to the rink. She

held the board upright against the rink's wooden frame, selected a nail, and started pounding the board into place. When she finished nailing the first board, she picked up a second, moved five feet farther down the rink, and started again.

It was hard work. Savannah prayed that it would pay off that night.

CHAPTER NINE

It took Savannah and her father most of the morning to circle the entire rink with boards. They took a short break for lunch, then went back outside. Mr. Smith handed Savannah a length of green pine garland and some red velvet ribbons. Savannah tied one end of the garland to a post, then moved to the next post and did the same thing. When she was through, the rink was ringed with green and red. Satisfied, Savannah took a quick shower and dressed for skating. She was out on the ice when her first guests arrived.

For the next hour, the Academy girls twirled, played tag, and helped each other up whenever someone fell down. Some of the parents joined them on the ice, but most preferred to stay inside, where it was warm. When the shadows started to lengthen, everyone else went inside, too. The girls grabbed some snacks, then gathered together in the living room and swapped gifts. Savannah was pleased to see that more than one girl traded the gift she'd opened for the bulb kit.

Angela sat next to Savannah. "Everything looks great!" she said enthusiastically. "I love the decorations you put up around the rink." She lowered her voice. "I keep forgetting to ask you. Is everything okay with Bizz?"

Savannah was about to reply when she heard the doorbell ring. A man called out, "Anybody home?" At the same time, another voice asked, "What are we doing *here?*"

Savannah's stomach did a flip-flop. "I'm about to find out," she replied to Angela. She got up and opened the front door. Jonas's father greeted her, and Alison stood next to him. Jonas, X, Charlie, Mark, and Bizz were behind them.

"Are we too early?" Mr. Malloy said, stepping into the house.

Savannah looked outside. While they'd been opening presents and eating, the sky had darkened to a deep midnight blue. "I'd say you're right on time." She beckoned them all inside.

Her classmates and their parents turned to look at the newcomers. Savannah cleared her throat nervously, then said, "Um, everyone? These are my friends. They've come to do some skating."

"Skating? It's pitch black outside!" X protested.

"Plus, I don't have my skates!" Jonas added.

"Who are all those girls?" Mark whispered hoarsely.

"I'm outta here," Bizz muttered. But before she could leave, Savannah grabbed her hand.

"Please," she said. "I want to show you something." Bizz blinked but allowed Savannah to pull her through the living room and out into the backyard. Everyone else followed.

The light from the house barely penetrated the darkness. Savannah dropped Bizz's hand and disappeared around the side of the house. There was a soft click and suddenly the skating rink was aglow. Twinkling white lights, hidden beneath the garland and ribbons, encircled the rink. Music piped in from unseen speakers.

Savannah reappeared. "I don't want to get all mushy or anything," she said, "but holidays are about friendship and togetherness, right? So I hope you'll all stay awhile longer and skate. Who knows? Maybe you'll make a new friend tonight."

CHAPTER TEN

Mr. Malloy produced a box filled with skates. "I collected these from your parents earlier this week," he said to his son and his son's friends.

"You knew about this?" Jonas cried as he dug into the box. "Why didn't you tell me?"

"What, and ruin Savannah's surprise?" Alison said. She tugged Jonas toward the ice. "Come on, shorty, close your mouth and move your feet."

"Shorty? Ha! I stand tall in these skates," Jonas retorted as he tied the laces. He stepped onto the rink, promptly lost his balance, and fell flat on the ice.

"From where I'm standing," Alison drawled, "you still seem short."

"Aw, just help me up," grumbled Jonas.

Savannah laughed. But her laughter died when she saw Bizz sitting alone on a bench. *Now's my chance,* she thought, walking over and sitting next to her friend.

"Hey. Wanna skate?"

"Too crowded," Bizz mumbled.

"Then can I give you your Christmas present?"

Bizz looked up. "You got me a Christmas present? What is it?"

Savannah reached under the bench and pulled out a colorfully wrapped present. "Open it."

Bizz peeled back the paper, then stared. "It's us!"

Savannah had framed a copy of the photo Alison took of them. She'd decorated the frame with tiny wooden snowboards, inline skates, and skateboards. On one side were the words "Friends to the end." She'd made similar frames for the others, too. Inside, she'd put copies of the snowball-fight pictures.

"It was dumb of me not to tell you about the school party," Savannah said. "I'm sorry. Can you forgive me?"

Bizz glanced at the photo one more time, then flung an arm around Savannah's shoulders. "Only if you'll forgive me for not showing up at the hill last weekend."

At Savannah's happy nod, Bizz grinned. "Good thing! Otherwise, you'll have to change what it says here!" She gave Savannah a squeeze.

"Hey you guys, c'mon!" Jonas called from the ice. "We're getting a game of hockey together!"

Savannah sighed. "I hope the Academy girls don't mind sharing the rink with hockey players," she said. But when she looked up, she saw that several Academy girls were holding hockey sticks and looking ready to play.

"Turns out some girls *do* like playing hockey." Angela appeared and handed each of them a stick. She kept one for herself. "Sarah's dad coaches a team. He had some sticks in his car."

Bizz raised her eyebrows. "I thought you said you'd never play hockey."

Angela grinned. "I can change my mind, can't I?"

"Sure," Bizz replied, "but don't expect me to take up figure skating!" Laughing, the two girls joined the others.

The party lasted another hour. After the last guest had left, Savannah helped her parents tidy up. Then, yawning, she headed for her room to change into her pajamas.

In the middle of her bed was a gift-wrapped box. Savannah sat down next to it and opened the card attached to the top. It was a Christmas card from Bizz and the others. Below their signatures Bizz had added a special note: "I hope you like these. I added a surprise to one of them. See if you can find it."

Savannah opened the box. Inside were a pair of blue-tinted goggles and a white fleece face warmer. It took her a moment to discover Bizz's surprise. When she did, her eyes welled with tears. Embroidered into the fleece in tiny blue letters were familiar words: "Friends to the end."

What Do You Need?

So you want to snowboard? Before you hit the slopes, you need the right equipment. New snowboards can be very expensive. However, you can save money by renting or borrowing a board or by purchasing a used board at a sports resale shop. Ask for help finding a board that suits your height, weight, and foot size. Short, lightweight people with small feet will do better with smaller, lighter, skinnier boards, for example. And be sure that the bindings are positioned correctly for your stance. Most right-handed boarders lead with their left foot. Lefties ride goofy foot, or right foot forward.

Boots are also a necessity. If your own winter boots fit the bindings and feel comfortable, you can use those. Otherwise, you can purchase special snowboarding boots. Both types should fit snugly around your ankle and heel. Loose-fitting boots make it more difficult to control the board when turning and stopping; they also let in the snow!

Now you're ready to suit up for the hill. You'll want to keep the heat in and the wet out, so dress in layers. Thermal long underwear made of wool or wool blends works well as a bottom layer. Fleece tops and pants are warm, flexible, and lightweight, making them good choices for a second layer. On top, wear snow pants and a jacket of water-resistant material. If you get hot while boarding, you can always remove one layer.

You should pay special attention to your hands, feet, head, and face. If you're boarding when it's very cold, wear two pairs of wool socks. Choose mittens or gloves that extend past your wrists, and seal out the snow with drawstrings. (Mittens keep fingers warmer than gloves do.) And be sure to wear a hat, since most body heat escapes through the top of the head. Finally, add a pair of ski goggles or sunglasses made with safety glass to block out the sun's glare and to prevent the wind from causing your eyes to tear up.

Now that you're all set with gear, you're ready to hit the slopes!